"I'll take this one," said Mr. Mac-Munn to the woman at the animal shelter. He had chosen the small gray dog called Cindy to become a hearing ear dog.

Hearing ear dogs are trained to alert their deaf owners to sounds the owners cannot hear. They learn to jump on the bed to awaken their owners when the alarm clock goes off, to bring their owners to the door when the bell rings, and to "tell" about other everyday sounds.

From the start, Cindy was a fast learner. But when the day came for her to meet her new owner, a teen-age girl, she didn't seem enthusiastic. So the girl had to win Cindy's affection before she could gain her help.

CINDY
A Hearing Ear Dog

CINDY
A Hearing Ear Dog

by Patricia Curtis

photographs by David Cupp

E. P. DUTTON   NEW YORK

The names of all the persons in the story of Cindy are fictitious, except for that of Donald P. MacMunn.

Library of Congress Cataloging in Publication Data

Curtis, Patricia.   Cindy, a hearing ear dog.

Summary: Describes the training of young dogs, selected from pounds and humane shelters, to help deaf owners by alerting them to sounds they cannot hear and providing companionship.
1. Hearing ear dogs—Juvenile literature. 2. Hearing ear dogs—Training—Juvenile literature. [1. Hearing ear dogs. 2. Dogs—Training] I. Cupp, David. II. Title.
HV2509.C87   636.7'086   80-24487   ISBN 0-525-27950-4

Published in the United States by Elsevier-Dutton Publishing Co., Inc., 2 Park Avenue, New York, N.Y. 10016

Published simultaneously in Canada by Clarke, Irwin & Company Limited, Toronto and Vancouver

Editor: Ann Troy   Designer: Claire Counihan

Printed in the U.S.A.   First Edition
10 9 8 7 6 5 4 3 2 1

Acknowledgments

We wish to thank the New England Education Center for the help and hospitality extended to us in the preparation of this book. We greatly appreciate the cooperation of the staff and students, particularly Donald P. MacMunn, Liz DeSantis, Gloria Place, Beth Thiele, and Bob Hine. Thanks also to Edward A. Zullo, D.V.M., and his staff at the Natick, Mass., Animal Clinic; to Lisa and Ann Acciaioli; and to our editor Ann Troy for her guidance and support.

Patricia Curtis
David Cupp

Foreword

"The dog is man's best friend" is an old cliché, but it has a ring of truth to it. The dog has been used in war and peace, at work on the farm and at home, and for years has guided the blind. Today, this intelligent animal takes on another role—helping the deaf!

And now, for once, we can help the dog. In our program for training hearing ear dogs, we take dogs from pounds and humane shelters and give them a new life with owners who will shower them with love and affection. These dogs are not only companions but serve their owners by alerting them to sounds they cannot hear. The hearing ear dog carries on the tradition of service.

Donald P. MacMunn, *Director*
Hearing Ear Dog Program
New England Education Center
Jefferson, Massachusetts

A small, fuzzy gray dog sat in the yard at an animal shelter and gazed out through the fence. She did this every day. She seemed to be watching and waiting for someone.

1

The dog had been found running all by herself along a busy road. A passerby had noticed her and brought her to safety at the shelter. She had no collar, no tags to show whose dog she was. Maybe she had fallen out the window of a moving car and gotten lost. Or maybe her owners had dumped her out of a car because they didn't want her anymore. She was very tired, cold, and hungry when she was found.

At first, the people at the shelter hoped that someone would come looking for the little dog. But days passed, and nobody came. She grew restless in her cage and in the fenced yard outside. She looked as if she were homesick. Some dogs seem content as long as they are cared for and can run about and play with other dogs. But most dogs really seem to need people. They appear to be happiest in homes, with owners who love them. Though the shelter people treated her kindly, this dog seemed sad. Whenever people came to the shelter to adopt a dog, she would look at them through the fence, as if she hoped they would take her.

One day, after a few weeks, a man came to the animal shelter looking for a dog to adopt. His name was Mr. MacMunn.

"I'm looking for a young, healthy, small- to medium-sized dog," said Mr. MacMunn. "It can be any breed, so long as it's smart and good-natured."

He stopped in front of the fuzzy gray dog's cage and looked carefully at her. She pricked up her ears and studied him hopefully.

"What's this one's name?" Mr. MacMunn asked the woman who was in charge of adoptions.

"We've been calling her Cindy," the woman answered. "She's a very nice dog—I think she might be what you're looking for."

"Here, Cindy," said Mr. MacMunn. Cindy came to the front of her cage, jumped up and down, and wagged her tail hard. She licked the man's hand through the bars of the cage.

"Could I take this one out of the cage, please?" asked Mr. MacMunn, and he let Cindy out. She put her front paws up on him and looked into his face as if she were saying "Please take me home!"

"I'll take this one," he said.

Cindy acted as if she were thrilled to be chosen. She jumped up and down some more, wagged her tail, and licked Mr. MacMunn's hands again. Mr. MacMunn patted her. He loved dogs.

He put her in his car and drove off. Cindy was excited at being out of the shelter. Maybe she thought she was going to a home at last. What Cindy didn't know was that before she would have an owner and a home of her own, she was going to school. She was going to be taught to be a hearing ear dog.

Most people have heard of guide dogs for the blind, such as Seeing Eye dogs. Few people know about hearing ear dogs. These dogs are trained to be helpers and companions to deaf people. The dogs alert their owners to certain sounds their owners can't hear.

Mr. MacMunn was the president of a college where he had started a special program to teach young men and women how to train dogs for the deaf. The students went to school for two years to learn to be professional hearing ear dog trainers. Then they were qualified for jobs in this work. And the dogs that they had trained were placed with deaf people who needed them.

When he arrived back at the college, Mr. MacMunn took Cindy into a building where a group of students were gathered. They petted and played with her for a while. Then Mr. MacMunn fed her with another new dog and put them in cages side by side. Cindy went to sleep.

The next morning, Mr. MacMunn took Cindy out of her cage. She leaped about him happily as he put a leash on her and led her out to his car again. "Where to, now?" Cindy probably wondered. She watched out the window as the car left the college and drove to a nearby town. It stopped in front of a white house with a sign out front that said Animal Clinic.

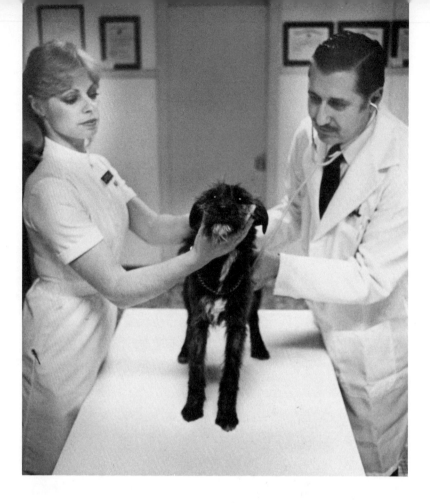

All dogs that enter the hearing ear dog training program at the college are first given a thorough checkup by a veterinarian to be sure they are healthy. Cindy seemed a little nervous when the veterinarian's assistant lifted her to the examining table, but she didn't struggle.

The doctor and his assistant were very patient and gentle. The doctor listened to Cindy's heart and lungs, felt her abdomen, took her temperature, looked in her eyes and throat and at her teeth. He checked her hair and skin. Everything okay so far. The doctor drew a sample of her blood so it could be examined at a laboratory. He also vaccinated her. Cindy endured all of this without a fuss.

Then the doctor gave special attention to Cindy's ears. This was perhaps the most important part of the examination. Her ears were going to have to hear for two—for herself and for the deaf person who would one day soon be her owner. Cindy's ears were fine.

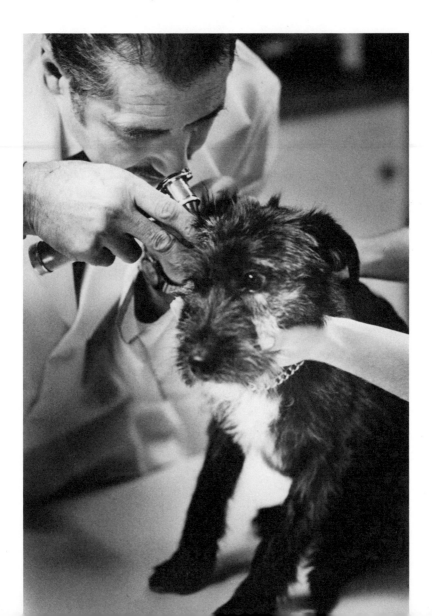

"This dog is in perfect health," said the vet to Mr. Mac-Munn.

But back at the college, Cindy had to pass one more test before she could be enrolled in the hearing ear dog training program. Mrs. Allen, the program director and teacher of kennel management, had to judge if Cindy would make a good pupil. Mrs. Allen would give Cindy a few basic lessons in obedience to see how the dog responded.

"Now, Cindy, I want you to sit when I tell you to," said the teacher.

Cindy looked up and wagged her tail. "Oh boy!" she seemed to say. "Are we going to play a game?"

"*Sit*, Cindy," commanded Mrs. Allen, pushing the dog into a sitting position and at the same time making a signal with her hand. In the future, Cindy would have to know to sit down when her owner spoke or simply made the hand signal.

Cindy had a little trouble with the command "Sit!" because she obviously wanted to jump and play. It was hard for her, but finally she learned to sit, at least for a few seconds, when she was told to.

Then Mrs. Allen went to one side of the room with Cindy, and another teacher went to the other.

"Come, Cindy!" said the other teacher, holding out her arms. Cindy ran to her, and the woman petted and praised her.

"*Come,* Cindy!" called Mrs. Allen, and Cindy bounded back across the room to her. She raced back and forth between Mrs. Allen and the other teacher whenever one of them said "*Come,* Cindy!"

Another part of the test was to learn to heel. This meant Cindy should walk beside Mrs. Allen while on the leash. If Cindy ran ahead or dragged behind, Mrs. Allen would say "*Heel,* Cindy!" and pull the dog beside her. This also seemed hard for Cindy. She wanted to play with the leash. But she also acted as if she wanted to please Mrs. Allen. And Cindy liked being praised and petted when she did the right thing. That was very important. It meant Cindy was eager to learn. Mrs. Allen knew dogs, and she decided Cindy could be trained. Cindy passed the test.

Cindy watched several other dogs who were brought into the room for their lessons. These were dogs who had been in the school for two or three weeks already and were no longer beginners. They were all young dogs, ranging in age from six or seven months to three years old. Most of them were quite small—not toy breeds, but not great big dogs either, because some of them would be given to deaf owners who lived in city apartments. Most of the dogs were mixed breeds, and many, like Cindy, had been adopted from animal pounds and shelters.

13

In the weeks that followed, Mrs. Allen and her students taught Cindy all the basic obedience commands and hand signals. Cindy had lessons for twenty minutes twice a day. She learned to come, heel, sit, stay, and lie down when she was told to. Two students, Lynn and Bill, also worked with Cindy. She learned to obey commands from them as well as from Mrs. Allen.

However, obeying was not the most important part of her training. The really hard lessons were still to come. To be a hearing ear dog, Cindy would have to learn to think

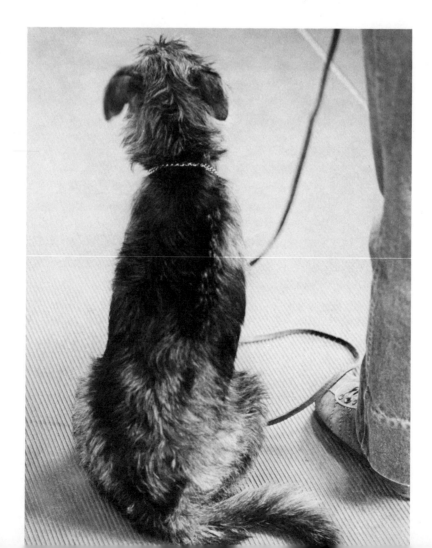

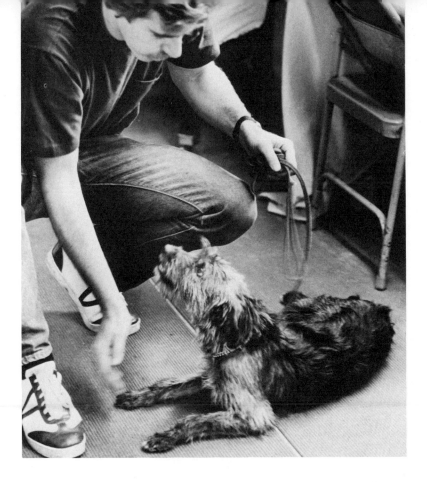

for herself when she heard certain sounds. A dog on whom a deaf person depends can't wait around for its owner to tell it what to do. When it hears a noise, it must figure out where the noise is and what it means. It must learn to bring its owner to the noise.

One morning, Mrs. Allen said Cindy had learned to obey so well that she was ready to be trained as a hearing ear dog. Lynn and Bill were assigned to teach her at the training cottage. The cottage had many different kinds of bells that could be rung during lessons, so the dogs could learn to respond to them.

The students began Cindy's training with the alarm clock. Lynn played the role of a deaf person. She lay down on a bed and set an alarm clock, while Bill stayed in the next room with Cindy on a leash. The alarm clock rang. Quickly, Bill brought Cindy to Lynn and encouraged the dog to jump up on the bed. Lynn, pretending to wake up, hugged Cindy and praised her.

After they did that exercise a few times, Bill let Cindy off the leash in the next room. *Dingdingding!* went the alarm clock.

"*Sound,* Cindy!" cried Bill. "Go *tell!*"

Cindy rushed into the bedroom, jumped up on the bed with Lynn, and kissed her, wiggling with joy. She seemed to love learning. Again, Lynn hugged her and told her she had done well. In a few days, Cindy learned always to make the right response to the alarm clock. In the future she would be able to tell her deaf owner an important piece of information: The alarm clock is ringing, it's time to get up.

19

In the hearing ear dog training program, dogs are never punished for making mistakes or not responding. But when they catch on and do the right thing, they are rewarded with praise and petting.

Bill and Lynn worked with Cindy for a short time every morning and again in the afternoon. If Cindy got tired during a lesson, they let her rest. But she seemed to enjoy these "games" with her teachers.

The next lesson Cindy learned was to tell Lynn when the doorbell rang. Most dogs will run to the door anyway whenever the bell rings. But a hearing ear dog must bring its owner to the door as well.

Bill went outside the cottage while Lynn put Cindy on a pulley that was attached to the door. Again, Lynn pretended to be the deaf person. When Bill rang the doorbell, Cindy of course ran to the door. "*Sound,* Cindy!" said Lynn. Then she used the pulley to lead Cindy back to her, saying, "*Tell,* Cindy!"

The training cottage had four different types of doorbells
which rang, buzzed, or chimed. Cindy learned them all.

Bill rang the doorbell again. "*Sound,* Cindy," said Lynn as Cindy ran to the door. "*Tell,* Cindy," she said, pulling Cindy back to her. Then she got up and went and opened the door.

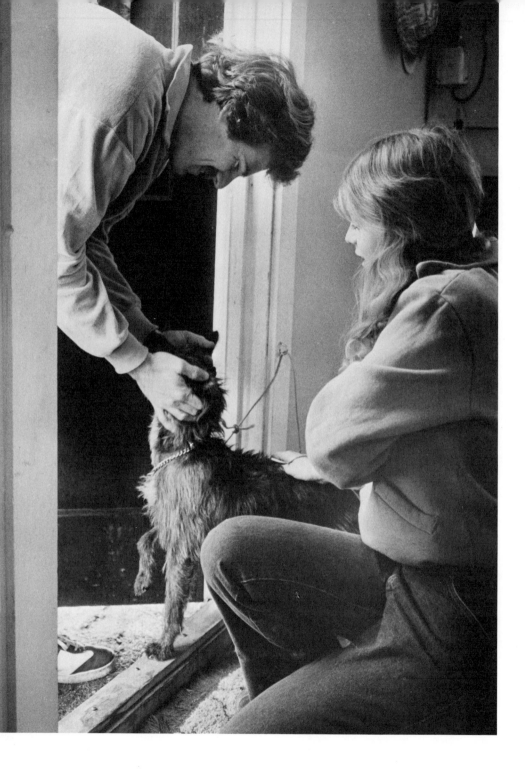

Cindy soon grasped the idea that when the doorbell rang, she was supposed to run back and forth between the door and "deaf" Lynn. She seemed pleased with herself when Lynn and Bill praised her.

Later, she also learned to tell Lynn when there was a knock at the door.

Over several weeks, Cindy learned to respond to other sounds too. When the teakettle on the stove began to sing, or when the oven timer buzzed, Cindy ran to tell Lynn or Bill and lead them to the sound. She also learned to tell them when the telephone rang. Most deaf people can't hear over a regular telephone, but some people who are only partly deaf can use special telephones.

Cindy learned fast. If she'd been given a report card, she would have earned all A's.

One day Lynn and Bill were told that an owner had been selected for Cindy—a deaf teenager named Jennifer. As soon as her junior high school classes were over for the summer, Jennifer would come to the college to meet Cindy and spend two weeks working with her. Jennifer would be taught to give commands and hand signals to Cindy. Cindy would learn to tell Jennifer instead of Lynn or Bill about the different sounds she knew. If all went well, Cindy would become Jennifer's hearing ear dog.

The big day arrived. Cindy, of course, knew nothing of the plans for her. She was taking a nap on the couch in the training cottage when Jennifer walked in. The dog opened her eyes and peeked out at the girl from between the pillows. Jennifer sat down and called Cindy to her. Cindy jumped off the couch and walked away, ignoring her. Jennifer was very disappointed.

Lynn knew American Sign Language, which many deaf people use, so she could communicate with Jennifer. "Don't feel bad," Lynn signed. "It always takes a little time for one of our dogs to get to know its new owner. After you have been taking care of Cindy for a few days, she'll come to you."

Cindy let Jennifer hug her, but she looked as if she were saying "How long do I have to put up with this pushy girl?"

When Jennifer gave Cindy her dinner that night, the dog warmed up to her a little. But Cindy probably believed she was Lynn and Bill's dog.

As the days passed, however, Cindy spent more and more time with Jennifer. She slept on the floor in Jennifer's room in the dormitory. Jennifer took her for walks. Jennifer had brought her bicycle to the college, and Cindy especially loved to run beside her when she rode it. Jennifer learned to bathe and brush the dog.

Without thinking about it, Cindy began to accept Jennifer as her owner.

The new dogs watched through a fence when Cindy and Jennifer went out together. Maybe they were wondering when their day would come and they would have owners too.

The next step was to teach Cindy to tell Jennifer instead of the trainers when the dog heard the sounds she had learned to respond to.

First they tried the doorbell. One trainer went outside the door while another stood behind Jennifer. When the bell rang, Cindy began to run back and forth between the door and the trainer.

"No, Cindy, *tell Jennifer!*" the trainer said.

They tried again. This time, Cindy ran to Jennifer. They kept up this lesson until Cindy always went to Jennifer when the doorbell rang. Then, they made the telephone ring, and sure enough, the dog ran to the girl and brought her to the phone. It was clear that Cindy was beginning to ally herself with Jennifer.

One very important bell that hearing ear dogs are taught to respond to is a smoke alarm that warns of fire. In the kitchen of the training cottage, there was such a bell. Of course, it could be made to ring without smoke. Lynn went into the kitchen with Cindy while Jennifer sat in the next room. Lynn made the smoke alarm go off.

34

"*Sound,* Cindy!" exclaimed Lynn. "*Tell Jennifer!*"

And Cindy dashed into the next room to Jennifer and led her out of the cottage.

Cindy's favorite bell was still the alarm clock. She
seemed to think it was so much fun to jump on the bed
and wake up Jennifer.

Jennifer of course had to learn her part too. Lynn taught
her to give Cindy all the obedience commands and hand
signals. Whenever Cindy responded correctly, Jennifer
hugged and petted her, just as the trainers had done.

The two weeks went by swiftly. The last few days, Jennifer's mother came and stayed at the college also. It was necessary for her to understand everything that Jennifer and Cindy knew. When they got home, Jennifer's mother would have to help Cindy do what she had learned at the college. She saw how Jennifer gave her dog the signals to come, sit, stay, lie down, and heel. And she watched while Cindy ran and fetched Jennifer whenever the doorbell, telephone, alarm clock, teakettle, oven timer, or smoke alarm sounded. Jennifer's mother was not deaf, but she used sign language with her daughter. Sometimes they signed "I love you" to each other.

The trainers also told Jennifer to watch Cindy when they were outdoors together. If Cindy pricked up her ears and turned her head, it would mean she heard a noise. Jennifer should then look to see what Cindy heard. It might be a siren, an automobile horn, a person shouting, an object falling onto the sidewalk—something going on that Jennifer should know about.

The trainers, especially Lynn and Bill, felt they would miss Cindy. But they had more dogs to teach to become hearing ear dogs for people who needed them.

Finally Jennifer packed up her suitcase, took Cindy by the leash, and walked out the door of the dormitory. Cindy at last had an owner who loved her. She was going to a home of her own, a home that really needed and wanted her.

More About
Hearing Ear Dogs

There are nearly two million totally deaf and over twelve million partly deaf people in the United States. Because of the success with guide dogs for the blind, it seemed a natural step to train hearing ear dogs for the deaf. The first to give the idea a try was a dog trainer named Agnes McGrath at the Minnesota Society for the Prevention of Cruelty to Animals. McGrath successfully trained several dogs in a pilot project in 1975.

McGrath went on to develop and direct the first systematic program for training hearing ear dogs at the American Humane Association in Denver. The idea caught on right away. Today, the institutions that train these dogs have a hard time filling the demand for them. Even so, the growth of programs has been slow—not from lack of applicants for dogs, but from lack of funding.

Directors of the most rigorous programs estimate that it costs $1,800 to $2,500 to train a dog. Some organizations are funded by donations and do not charge for the dogs. At others, fees vary. Deaf people who can't afford the regular fees are sometimes allowed to pay less. Some places help deaf people train their own dogs to become hearing ear dogs.

Some agencies will not train a dog for anyone under the age of eighteen. They believe adults need the dogs more, because children usually live with their families, who provide help and protection. Other places have no age restrictions.

An owner is usually chosen for a dog before, or at some point during, the animal's training. The dog may then receive special instruction according to the individual needs of the future owner. For instance, some hearing ear dogs are taught to respond to a baby crying. Or, if the owner is totally deaf, telephone training is not needed.

In some programs, a trainer accompanies each trained dog to the new owner's home and stays for three to five days or more, helping the animal and family adjust to one another. Other institutions, like the college where Cindy was trained, have found it works better to have the new owner come to the dog. The owner learns to work with the dog at the place where the dog was trained.

Since deaf people would not be able to hear an intruder, the dogs offer protection in households in which no member hears. Mainly, however, their role is not protection but assistance. They make it possible for deaf people to be more independent.

In the early days of the work with these dogs, trainers worried that the animals would forget their training if they lived with deaf owners in households with others who could hear. If another member of the family answered the doorbell or took the teakettle off the stove, would the dog stop telling its owner? Interestingly, the animals themselves settled that question. They ignore the sounds when the hearing members of the family are home, but take over when they're alone with the deaf persons.

Because hearing ear dogs are new, it is not yet known how much they can do. All of them are intelligent, but some may be smarter than others. Some dogs may forget or grow lazy. Some owners may undo their dogs' training; still other people may teach their dogs far more than the animals were trained to do.

Some thirty-two states now allow hearing ear dogs in the same public places (buses, post offices, stores, etc.) that guide dogs for the blind are permitted. One way to identify hearing ear dogs is by the blaze orange collar or harness they wear.

So far, most people involved with them believe hearing ear dogs can provide much help for deaf people. And they give something else everybody needs—love!

Here are some of the organizations that have training programs for hearing ear dogs:

- American Humane Association, 5351 S. Roslyn St., Englewood, Colorado 80111. (303) 779–1400
- Audio Dogs, 27 Crescent St., Brooklyn, New York 11208. (212) 827–2792
- Dogs for the Deaf, Applegate Behavior Station, 13260 Highway 238, Jacksonville, Oregon 97530. (503) 899–7177 or (503) 899–7542
- Guide Dog Foundation, 371 Jericho Turnpike, Smithtown, New York 11787. (516) 265–2121
- Hearing Dog, Inc., Agnes McGrath, director; 5901 E. 89 Ave., Henderson, Colorado 80640. (303) 287–3277 (voice/TTY)
- New England Education Center, Hearing Ear Dog Program, Bryant Hill Farm, 76 Bryant Rd., Jefferson, Massachusetts 01522. (617) 829–9745
- San Francisco SPCA, Hearing Dog Program, 2500 Sixteenth St., San Francisco, California 94103. (415) 621–2174 (voice/TTY)

This organization teaches deaf people to train their own dogs:

- Handi-Dogs, Inc., P.O. Box 12563, Tucson, Arizona 85732. (602) 326–3412 or (602) 325–6466

49

Index